Beach Day!

by Candice Ransom

illustrated by Erika Meza

Random House 🏠 New York

Summer morning.

Dear Parents:

Congratulations! Your child is taking the first steps on an exciting journey. The destination? Independent reading!

STEP INTO READING® will help your child get there. The program offers five steps to reading success. Each step includes fun stories and colorful art or photographs. In addition to original fiction and books with favorite characters, there are Step into Reading Non-Fiction Readers, Phonics Readers and Boxed Sets, Sticker Readers, and Comic Readers—a complete literacy program with something to interest every child.

Learning to Read, Step by Step!

Ready to Read   Preschool–Kindergarten
• big type and easy words • rhyme and rhythm • picture clues
For children who know the alphabet and are eager to begin reading.

Reading with Help   Preschool–Grade 1
• basic vocabulary • short sentences • simple stories
For children who recognize familiar words and sound out new words with help.

Reading on Your Own   Grades 1–3
• engaging characters • easy-to-follow plots • popular topics
For children who are ready to read on their own.

Reading Paragraphs   Grades 2–3
• challenging vocabulary • short paragraphs • exciting stories
For newly independent readers who read simple sentences with confidence.

Ready for Chapters   Grades 2–4
• chapters • longer paragraphs • full-color art
For children who want to take the plunge into chapter books but still like colorful pictures.

STEP INTO READING® is designed to give every child a successful reading experience. The grade levels are only guides; children will progress through the steps at their own speed, developing confidence in their reading. The F&P Text Level on the back cover serves as another tool to help you choose the right book for your child.

Remember, a lifetime love of reading starts with a single step!

For Patricia, who loves the beach!
—C.R.

To Jude, who made me feel at home away from home
—E.M.

Text copyright © 2020 by Candice Ransom
Cover art and interior illustrations copyright © 2020 by Erika Meza

Visit us on the Web!
StepIntoReading.com
rhcbooks.com

Educators and librarians, for a variety of teaching tools, visit us at RHTeachersLibrarians.com

Library of Congress Cataloging-in-Publication Data
Names: Ransom, Candice F., author. | Meza, Erika, illustrator.
Title: Beach day! / by Candice Ransom ; illustrated by Erika Meza.
Description: First edition. | New York : Random House Children's Books,
[2020] | Series: Step into reading. Step 1, Ready to read | Audience:
Ages 4–6. | Audience: Grades K–1. | Summary: A family spends a fun day
at the beach, collecting shells, building sandcastles, and flying kites.
Identifiers: LCCN 2019027016 (print) | LCCN 2019027017 (ebook) |
ISBN 978-1-5247-2043-8 (trade) | ISBN 978-1-5247-2044-5 (lib. bdg.) |
ISBN 978-1-5247-2045-2 (ebook)
Subjects: CYAC: Stories in rhyme. | Beaches—Fiction.
Classification: LCC PZ8.3.R1467 Be 2020 (print) | LCC PZ8.3.R1467 (ebook) |
DDC [E]—dc23

Printed in the United States of America
10 9 8
First Edition

This book has been officially leveled by using the F&P Text Level Gradient™ Leveling System.

Pack the car.

Follow beach road.

Here we are!

Spread out blanket.

Set up chairs.

Shoo the gulls
into the air!

Hot sand!

Run fast!

Dive in quick!

Something tickles.
Seaweed—ick!

Hold my hand.

Be very brave.

One, two, three—now!
Jump that wave!

Along the beach,
pick up shells.

Most are pretty.

This one smells!

Getting hungry.

Time to eat.

Ice cream sandwich,
cool and sweet.

Shovels,

buckets.

Dig by the sea.

Build a castle
tall as me.

Look what I found!

Watch your toe.

Mister Crab,
back you go!

Climb the steep hill.

Wind just right.

Let out long string.

Fly our kite!

Sun is setting,
almost dark.

Fun rides,

more treats
in the park.

Turning wheel soars
in the air.
Cotton candy
in your hair!

Giant moon looks

like a peach.

Best day ever!
Goodbye, beach!